W9-AAQ-999

Dear Reader:

How big do you think the world's biggest lobster is?

A boy in Nova Scotia (Canada) found a 44-pound lobster in 1977. (It was later sold to a restaurant in the United States.)

While not as gigantic as that, Captain Nemo, the lobster in this story, isn't exactly tiny. Ivy Higgins doesn't want to sell the big, 27-pound lobster her father has in his fish store. She adopts him as her friend, and ...well, you'll see.

Look through Guinness Book of World Records or a similar book. What other world's biggest things can you find? It's fun!

Sincerely,

Stephen Fraser

Stephen Fraser
Senior Editor
Weekly Reader Books

THE LOBSTER
and IVY HIGGINS

Weekly Reader Book Club Presents

The Lobster
and Ivy Higgins

Nancy Buss
Illustrated by Kim Mulkey

CAROLINE HOUSE

This book is a presentation of Newfield Publications, Inc.
Newfield Publications offers book clubs for children
from preschool through high school. For further
information write to: **Newfield Publications, Inc.,**
4343 Equity Drive, Columbus, Ohio 43228.

Published by arrangement with Caroline House.
Newfield Publications is a trademark
of Newfield Publications, Inc. Weekly Reader
is a federally registered trademark of
Weekly Reader Corporation.

Text copyright © 1992 by Nancy Buss
Illustrations copyright © 1992 by Kim Mulkey

All rights reserved
Published by Caroline House
Boyds Mills Press, Inc.
A Highlights Company
910 Church Street
Honesdale, Pennsylvania 18431

Publisher Cataloging-in-Publication Data
Buss, Nancy.
The lobster and Ivy Higgins / by Nancy Buss ; illustrated by Kim Mulkey.
[64]p.: col. Ill. ; cm.
Summary: Ivy Higgins wants to keep the twenty seven pound lobster her
father has in his fish store. Her efforts to save the lobster make for a heart-
warming story.
ISBN 1-56397-011-2
1. Lobsters—Juvenile fiction. [1. Lobsters—Fiction.] I. Mulkey, Kim, ill.
II. Title.
[F]   1992
Library of Congress Catalog Card Number: 91-72868

First edition, 1992
Book designed by Charlotte Staub

Distributed by St. Martin's Press
Printed in the United States of America

For Don,
my best friend, my patron, my husband.

CHAPTER 1

They were chasing her again. Ivy Higgins could hear their yells echoing behind her.

"Poison Ivy, smells so bad. Stinks of fish guts like her dad!"

Ivy ducked in the alley between Peterson's General Store and Fetzner's Bait and Tackle Shop. She hid behind the milk crates until her third-grade classmates disappeared.

"Stupid jerks!" she whispered.

Ivy had been hiding one place or another since first grade, when the kids in her class learned that her father owned the Hanford Corners Fish Market.

Ivy sniffed her fingers, then her jacket. They both smelled faintly of fish.

"A good clean odor," her father always told her. Well, not to the kids at school it wasn't. If they weren't calling her Poison Ivy, they were calling her Fish Breath or Shark Spit.

Ivy carefully looked over the milk crates, then tiptoed out of the alley. Jerome Flensted and his buddies were gone, so Ivy sped the rest of the way home. She dashed up the back stairs and headed for the refrigerator. As she pulled out a carton of lemon yogurt, she heard her father on the telephone in the next room. His voice was filled with excitement. Ivy peeked around the corner.

"How big?" he asked as he paced back and forth. Then he whistled. "Twenty-seven pounds! And how long?" There was a pause. "That's the biggest one ever caught around Rocky Cove!"

Ivy groaned. Fish! Big deal! She sat down at the

table and took a spoonful of yogurt, letting the sweet-sour taste fill her mouth. She couldn't understand how he could be excited about a fish when he sold them all day.

Ivy lowered her spoon. He didn't *usually* get so excited. Something special was going on. Ivy was just about to get up again when her father came bursting into the room.

"Wait till you hear!" he said. "That was Tom Robinson. He just pulled into Rocky Cove with a twenty-seven-pound lobster!"

Ivy's brown eyes widened. No wonder her father was excited. "It must be . . . ." She held out her skinny arms, trying to guess its size.

"Thirty-two inches long," said Mr. Higgins. "Grab your jacket. We're going to pick it up."

Ivy's mouth dropped open. "It's coming *here*?"

Her father nodded. Then he picked her up and whirled her in the air, just as he had when she was little. Both of them were breathless with laughter when he set her down. Her father gasped for air. "Do you know how many people will come see that lobster?"

"Millions!" Ivy said.

Her father chuckled. "Not that many. But things should really pick up around here."

Ivy grinned. Business had been slow ever since the supermarket on the edge of town had added its own fish market. But Super Food wouldn't have a twenty-seven-pound lobster to display. Ivy couldn't wait to see it.

It took a half hour to drive to Rocky Cove, where their friend Tom Robinson moored his fishing boat. For the first few blocks Ivy sat low in her seat. She could barely see out the window.

"Sit up straight," her father said.

Ivy sighed. "I've been doing that all day," she complained, staying where she was. "I'd just like to relax for a while."

But Ivy was far from relaxed—she was hiding again. She hated it when the kids from school saw her in the beat-up truck with its dented fenders and moldy green paint. It was one more thing they could use to torment her. But she couldn't tell her father. He'd give her his sad look and his lecture about people being more important than things.

Ivy knew he was right, but what her father didn't know was just how mean some kids could be.

CHAPTER 2

Once outside of town, Ivy sat up. The bouncing, swaying truck became as much fun as a carnival ride. It always made her giggle, even on the worst of days. And she loved visiting Tom Robinson. She wished she and her father could live in Rocky Cove, where there were boats and waves and sea gulls—and where all the kids were used to the smell of fish.

When they arrived at the pier, Ivy saw the *TV 8 News* car.

"Hey, look," she said.

Her father nodded. "Tom said he had called the newspaper and the TV stations. Sure enough, they've sent a camera crew."

Ivy could see people gathered in front of Tom's boat. Among them were a cameraman and a reporter with a microphone.

"Come on, kiddo," her father said. "Let's see this monster I've bought!"

Ivy quickly slid over the cracked plastic seat and followed her father down the pier, around the fish shanties and lobster pots. Sea gulls screamed overhead, announcing their arrival.

Tom Robinson waved to them, his weathered face crinkling in a grin. "Here's the proud owner now."

The cameraman turned toward them, and the reporter pushed the microphone at Ivy's father. "I understand you've bought this lobster, Mr. Higgins. What are your plans for it?"

Ivy's father cleared his throat and smoothed his wispy hair. "Well, first I'd like to see him. Then he's going on display at my fish market—the

Hanford Corners Fish Market. Everyone can get a good look at him there."

Ivy heard an unfamiliar tremor in his voice. But at least her father had managed to say something. If they had asked her anything, she would have been too frightened to speak.

The crowd parted as Ivy and her father walked to the edge of the pier. Tom Robinson bent down and held the lobster up. It was the biggest lobster Ivy had ever seen! The enormous front claws waved in the air a few inches above the fisherman's head. Its fanlike tail hung down past Tom's waist.

Tom winked at her. "He's almost as big as you are. Why, he could be up to a hundred years old! Look at those barnacles growing on him."

The reporter scowled as Ivy, her shyness forgotten, came closer and felt the sharp, stonelike barnacles with the tips of her fingers. "They're just like the ones that grow on the pier."

The fisherman nodded. "Same creatures. I guess they'll attach themselves to darn near anything."

"Look," said the reporter. "Can you talk about this later? I've got to get this tape back to the studio. Let's get a shot of you two guys and the lobster," he said, waving Ivy away.

But Tom grabbed Ivy's arm. "I think you'll need a shot of all three of us," he said. "After all, Ivy here will be taking care of this big fellow."

The reporter scowled again but nodded to the cameraman, who filmed the scene. "There. That's a wrap! We're outta here!"

CHAPTER 3

Tom Robinson motioned to Ivy as he poured some coffee for her father and Mr. Jacobs from the *Hanford Corners Gazette*. "Come see this great beast," he said.

Ivy quickly joined him. "How did you catch him?" she asked. "He's too big to fit in the traps."

Tom took a slurp of coffee and straightened his stained baseball cap. "This guy's too big for any lobster pot. I snagged him with my net, fishing for cod."

Ivy stared at the lobster as Tom began to cover the huge crustacean with wet burlap to keep it comfortable.

Her father and Mr. Jacobs joined them.

"So what are you going to name him, Ivy?" her father asked.

"Captain Nemo," she said quickly, remembering the video her father had rented last week.

"Captain Nemo it is," said Mr. Jacobs. "It will be in tomorrow's paper." He quickly snapped their picture.

When they arrived home, Ivy helped her father set up the large tank in the front window of the fish market.

The Captain seemed more comfortable once he was back in the water. He settled to the bottom of the tank and crawled forward on his four pair of walking legs. His antennae waved back and forth in the bubble stream created by the pump as he explored his cramped new home. His eyestalks turned one way, then another.

Ivy tapped the side of the glass with a chewed fingernail. "He's looking at me," she said.

Her father didn't hear. He was busy putting up a sign in the window. CAPTAIN NEMO—THE EIGHTH WONDER! it proclaimed.

He *is* a wonder, Ivy thought. She went over to the glass display cooler that ran the length of her father's market. She took out a raw shrimp and tossed it over the side of the tank. It sank to the bottom, where the Captain scooped it toward his mouth with one large claw and ate it greedily.

"Just wait till the kids at school hear about you!" Ivy said. "And wait till I tell them about the TV and the newspaper!" Suddenly she couldn't wait for tomorrow.

The next morning Ivy skipped breakfast. She dashed downstairs to say good-bye to her father and the Captain. "I'll be back soon," she whispered. "I'm going to tell the whole third grade about you. You'll be famous, Captain!"

Someday I'm going to be famous too, she thought as she headed for school. But I'll probably have to change my name. Whoever heard of anyone famous named Ivy? Whitney was a good name, or Angelica. Anything but Ivy.

She had once looked up her name in the *Name Your Baby* book that she had found in the bottom of the bookcase and discovered that it meant "A plant or a vine." Well who wanted to be named after a plant? She might as well be called Watermelon or Tomato. No wonder the kids in her class laughed at her. None of them were named for plants!

"Clarissa," she said to herself. "Clarissa Higgins." That was nice. She could be rich and famous with a name like that. "Clarissa Higgins," she whispered once more as she entered her classroom.

CHAPTER 4

"Here comes old Fish Breath," Jerome Flensted said. "And there goes the fresh air!" He sat behind Ivy and poked her sharply between the shoulder blades.

Ivy pulled forward in her seat and tried to ignore the snickering laughter that skittered about her ears. Just wait till they heard about the Captain!

But how was she going to tell them? She hated show and tell! Every time she had to stand up in front of the class, her mind became a blank, and her knees and voice shook just like her grandfather's. People said he had palsy, but Ivy wondered if he had just done too many show and tells when he was in school.

Still, she tried to tell herself, this wasn't the same. She could talk from her seat. She could do that! So right after the Pledge of Allegiance, Ivy raised her hand.

Mrs. Turner smiled. "Yes, Ivy?"

"I . . . uh . . . I have a new pet," she said. "It's a twenty-seven-pound lobster named Captain Nemo." Ivy talked fast so she would get all her words out before her brain stopped.

She heard Jerome snort behind her. "Sure you do," he said. "If you bring it in, I'll bring my spotted hippo!"

The class laughed, and Ivy felt her cheeks burn. She whirled around in her seat. "It's true!" she shouted. "His picture will be in tonight's paper and on *TV 8 News*, too!"

Ivy's voice was almost drowned out with the laughter, but *everyone* heard Mrs. Turner.

She smacked a ruler, hard, against her desk. "Quiet!" she said. "Ivy, turn around! Now, everyone get busy with those math problems. Ivy, come up here."

Ivy felt everyone looking at her as she walked to the teacher's desk. Mrs. Turner spoke quietly, but Ivy knew the whole front row could hear.

"It's not good to make up stories to get attention, Ivy."

"But, Mrs. Turner, I . . ."

"Go back to your seat. I don't want to hear any more about it!"

Ivy blinked quickly. She couldn't cry now. It would make things worse. She returned to her seat without looking at anyone. She took out her math book and pretended to work, pulling herself forward so Jerome couldn't poke her with his pencil. She ignored the kicks she felt on the bottom of her seat.

At lunch, Ivy felt sick to her stomach. She went to the nurse's office, where her father picked her up at one-thirty.

"We'll get you right into bed," he said as he

hurried to the truck. "Some peppermint tea, and you'll be as good as new."

But Ivy didn't think she'd ever feel good again. She had expected Jerome and the others to laugh. But she hadn't expected Mrs. Turner not to believe her. Mrs. Turner had always been her friend. She never allowed the kids to tease her in class. Once she had even made Jerome stay after school when he had held his nose as Ivy took her turn at reading. Now Ivy felt betrayed. And she cried herself to sleep.

CHAPTER 5

Ivy was awakened by her father. "I thought you'd like to see this," he said, showing her the front page of the afternoon paper.

Ivy sat up and rubbed her eyes. There they were, Ivy, her father, Tom Robinson, and the Captain, grinning at the world from a large picture. Below it she read, "Rocky Cove Fisherman Catches a Big One." Then it told how the Captain had been captured, that he could be seen at her father's fish market, and—just as Mr. Jacobs had promised—

that "Ivy Higgins has named the lobster Captain Nemo."

"All right!" said Ivy.

"I thought it would make you feel better," her father said. "Now, how about some soup? The news is almost on. We can eat in the living room so we won't miss it."

Ivy quickly got out of bed and wolfed down not only a bowl of soup, but three tuna sandwiches before their story appeared. Then suddenly there they were, just like in the paper, only now they were talking and moving—and in full color! The story was over quickly, but Ivy had recorded it, and she watched it over and over.

That night Ivy had a hard time sleeping. At five the next morning, she quietly crept downstairs and entered the fish market. Light from the streetlamp filtered through the window in a silver stream. Ivy could see Captain Nemo's huge bulk filling the tank. She tiptoed over, stopping to pick up three raw shrimp on the way. She dropped them with a plop into the water and watched as the Captain ate them.

"You looked good on TV, Captain," she whispered. "We both did! I can't wait to see what Mrs. Turner says now. And here's your picture in the paper. I'll bet nobody even showed you!"

The lobster's antennae waved an answer in the bubbling water. His eyestalks twitched back and forth.

"Dad said I can invite the whole class to see you."

But later that morning when she entered her classroom, she was afraid to ask. She could feel her heart beating as she took her seat. Maybe they wouldn't want to come. Maybe they'd laugh at her father, too. She wished everyone would stop staring at her.

Finally Mrs. Turner spoke. "Ivy, we owe you an apology. I'm sorry we didn't believe you yesterday. It's just that none of us had ever heard of a lobster that big!"

Ivy smiled, then quickly lowered her eyes. She felt her face getting warm again. She tried to tell them about her father's invitation, but no words would come.

Her stomach started churning again. If she didn't ask them, her father would wonder why. She couldn't tell him how they treated her. For a moment she missed her mother very much.

Ivy hadn't felt so lonely when her mother was alive. The kids had still teased her, but her mother had listened to her troubles and made her feel good again. But she couldn't tell her father. He would have gone down to the school and made a big fuss. That never helped. Ivy knew it was better to handle her own problems, but that was getting harder.

Ivy heard her name again and looked up to find Mrs. Turner still talking.

"Mr. Higgins called the school this morning, inviting us to see Captain Nemo tomorrow. I think it's a wonderful idea!"

Everyone stared at Ivy once more, but this time they were smiling. She shyly smiled back. Then she felt a kick on the back of her seat. "I'm bringing a clothespin for my nose," Jerome whispered.

CHAPTER 6

That night Ivy helped her father get ready for her class's visit. She swept the floor and shined the glass display case and the Captain's tank until they glistened. Her father baked cookies and mixed up three pitchers of lemonade.

But on the way to school the next day, Ivy was afraid. What if her class laughed at her father's store, with its sawdust-covered floors and the white paper signs in the window? What if they didn't like the Captain? What if . . .?

"Everything will be fine," her father had said earlier. But that didn't help. Ivy felt she would explode as she sat at her desk and tried to work.

But at last it was time to go, and Ivy got to walk up front with Mrs. Turner. Ivy felt relieved. At least she didn't have to walk with Jerome, who had tried to pinch her all morning with the clothespin he had brought for his nose.

Ivy felt even better when they got to the market. No one laughed at her father or his store. Everyone crowded around the tank and admired the Captain. Even Jerome seemed excited when he saw the huge creature.

"Wow!" he said. "What a monster! He must be the biggest lobster in the world!" He tapped the glass with the clothespin. "Boy! Are you lucky!" he said, turning to Ivy. It was the first nice thing he had ever said to her.

"Is it a boy or a girl lobster?" Mary Anne Costanza wanted to know.

"A boy lobster, of course!" said Jerome.

Mr. Higgins nodded. "Jerome's right," he said.

"What does he eat?" Richard Fairbrother asked.

"Shrimp and clams, and other small shellfish," Ivy's father answered.

The questions went on and on until Mrs. Turner said it was time to go.

The students groaned, then gave a cheer as Ivy's father told them about the lemonade and the cookies.

"Well, just this once," Mrs. Turner said.

Ivy couldn't stop smiling as she helped her father pour the drinks. Things had gone better than she had hoped. No one had said one bad thing. Even Jerome had been excited and had not teased her for once. So when her father announced the news, she wasn't ready.

"I have a surprise," he said. "Even Ivy doesn't know about this. In two weeks, the Chamber of Commerce will hold a special raffle as part of its annual Fall Festival. First prize is a clambake for fifty. The Chamber will supply the clams, corn, and chickens, and I'm donating Captain Nemo himself!" He handed a blue raffle ticket to each child. "Here's a free chance for each of you. Of course, your families are welcome to buy more."

The children all clapped, and there were a few whistles. Everyone seemed excited except Ivy and Jerome.

Ivy simply stood and stared dumbly at her father. "The Captain?" she said. For a minute she didn't seem to understand. Then she knew!

"No!" she shouted. "He's mine! You can't raffle him off for people to eat!" Her body was stiff with anger. How dare he do such a thing to the Captain!

She could feel the tears well up in her eyes. She didn't care if she cried in front of the class or not. He just couldn't do this horrible thing!

The only sound in the market was the bubbling water in the Captain's tank.

"Let's have two straight lines," Mrs. Turner said. "It's time to go."

Only Jerome remained where he was.

"Jerome, please get a partner and line up."

Jerome grabbed Ivy's hand and pulled her into line. "Come on, Fish Breath," he whispered.

Ivy was too miserable to protest. She didn't want to go back to school. But she couldn't stay home with her father, either. She wanted to run away somewhere. But then who would protect the Captain?

She would, that's who! She would fight them all! She twisted out of Jerome's grip. She would start by not holding hands with the enemy!

CHAPTER 7

All the way back to school, Jerome kept pestering her, but Ivy refused to listen. "Just shut up, Jerome!" She said it so loudly that Mrs. Turner gave her a warning look.

Back in school, Jerome started in again. "Psst," he said, poking her in the back.

Ivy moved forward in her seat.

Later, he slipped a note onto her desk as he went to sharpen his pencil.

Ivy angrily ripped it in half before she noticed there was something inside. Jerome's raffle ticket. What was he up to? She watched him as he returned to his seat, expecting to see his usual smirk. Instead he was frowning, and he seemed worried. She looked again at the note, pushing the torn pieces together.

We have to save the Captain, it said. Meet me after school.

No way! Ivy thought. He's just being mean again. Still, he did seem to like the Captain. All the kids did. Maybe he meant what he wrote. If he would help her, maybe . . .

She shook her head in confusion. Nobody will help. No one even likes me. Still . . .

Ivy decided it was worth a risk. Saving the Captain was more important than anything!

After school she made herself wait until Jerome came outside. When he appeared she hugged her books tightly and bit her lip.

At first, fumbling in his backpack, he didn't say anything. He smiled when he found what he was looking for. "Here," he said, shoving a small bundle of blue tickets at her. "I collected them from everyone in the class during lunch."

Ivy looked at the bundle of raffle tickets. She didn't know what to say.

"But why?" Her voice trailed off.

Jerome looked at her as if she were crazy. "'Cause that lobster's the greatest thing I've ever seen! I can't believe your father's going to let him be eaten!"

"Me neither," Ivy said quietly.

"Maybe if you tell him we don't want his rotten old tickets, he'll cancel the raffle."

"Maybe," she said.

But when she got home, she could tell it wouldn't work. The store was crowded with people, and the big glass bowl was half-filled with blue ticket stubs.

She rushed upstairs to her room, ignoring her father's friendly wave. When he called her for supper, she didn't answer.

"Ivy, we've got to talk about this," he said, coming into her room.

She turned away.

"Ivy, I own a fish market. All the fish in the store are bought to be eaten."

She sat up, angrily pushing away his hand. "But Captain Nemo is special," she said. "You let me name him and everything!"

"I didn't know you thought he was yours," said her father. "I'd like to be able to give him to you, but I can't afford to. And I've already promised him to the Chamber."

"I could get a paper route, or do chores, and buy him back," Ivy said.

Her father shook his head. "I've gone too far with the raffle. We've sold over three hundred tickets. And the raffle is bringing in business. We need that, Ivy. Besides, we can't keep the Captain very long in that tank. He's too big. He's used to the whole ocean. It's not fair to keep him in such a tiny place."

Ivy turned back to the wall. "It's not fair to eat him, either!"

CHAPTER 8

After school the next day, Ivy met Jerome. "My dad won't cancel the raffle," she said. "And he won't let me buy the Captain back."

"Maybe we can *win* him back," Jerome said.

"What do you mean?"

Jerome rubbed his hands together. "Look, we have twenty-three tickets from our class. That gives us a lot better chance of winning than if we had only one ticket apiece. And if we collect more tickets, we increase our chances."

Ivy felt excited. "What if we made some posters and asked everyone in the school to donate their tickets to help save the Captain? Do you think they'd let us put up posters in the hall?"

Jerome's brown eyes sparkled. "Maybe in every room. With that many tickets, we'll just have to win! Maybe we could even go door to door."

Ivy felt her stomach quiver. She didn't talk easily to strangers. Going door to door would be like doing a show and tell over and over again. But Jerome was right. The more tickets they had, the safer the Captain would be. She'd have to do it!

That weekend she and Jerome made signs, and on Monday morning Ivy got permission to take one to each classroom. The kindergarten and first and second grades were easy. But when she entered the fourth, fifth, and sixth grades, her tongue suddenly became too big for her mouth, and her sweaty hands made her posters all wrinkled. By the time she got to Mr. Lenzi's fifth grade, she felt as if her stomach had turned to stone. To make matters worse, when Mr. Lenzi saw her posters, he wanted her to give a speech!

Ivy shook her head, but before she knew it she was standing in front of the class. Mr. Lenzi stood behind her with his hands resting lightly on her shoulders. There was no escape! At first she did nothing but stare at the floor. Then Mr. Lenzi said, "I'm sure you've all heard about the lobster that was caught a few days ago. I know some of you have bought raffle tickets. Well, Ivy has something to ask you."

Ivy started to stammer and trip over her words, afraid of the big kids who stared at her. She could almost hear them laughing. But suddenly she thought how the Captain would look, all boiled and red on a platter. She took a deep breath and began.

When she finished, three kids gave her tickets, and the rest promised theirs by the end of the week. When she left the room, she was shaking, but she couldn't wait to tell Jerome!

After school that day, she and Jerome scoured the nearby streets, knocking on doors and telling people about the Captain. Some people didn't answer, and others who did, didn't listen. But by the end of the day they had collected thirty-eight more tickets.

"If we split up we could cover twice the number of houses tomorrow," Jerome said.

Ivy started to say no, but once more she thought of the Captain, and the next day she went to the houses by herself. She came home with twenty-nine tickets.

Jerome met her at the market. They raced upstairs to count their treasure. "That makes one hundred and sixty-three!" Jerome said, as he finished counting the pile on top of the table.

"One hundred and sixty-three what?" asked Ivy's father, who had just come into the kitchen.

Jerome held up a handful of blue stubs. "We're going to win the Captain!" Jerome said. "Then we'll put him back in the ocean and he won't be eaten."

Ivy's father sighed. "Oh, Ivy. This isn't going to work."

"It will!" said Ivy. "I've already asked Tom Robinson if he'd take the Captain back. He said yes."

Her father sighed again. "OK, I give up," he said. "I really hope you guys do win. I don't want the Captain cooked either. But this isn't the way to rescue him."

"How then?" asked Ivy.

"I wish I knew," said Mr. Higgins.

CHAPTER 9

Fall Festival Day dawned bright and clear, and Ivy was glad it had finally arrived. The last week with her father had been hard. The fate of the Captain had hung between them like a stone. Ivy hadn't known what to do with all the love and anger she felt. She knew her father was a good man and would have saved the Captain if he could. Yet it was his fault that this had happened. Her feelings were all mixed up like a fish stew. But today would

see the end of it. They would win the Captain, and Tom Robinson would return him to the sea, where he belonged.

The sound of feet pounding up the back stairs interrupted her thoughts. Jerome flew through the door.

"Come on, Fish Breath. We haven't hit the streets behind the school yet."

Ivy grabbed her jacket and led the way.

"Let's see the Captain first," Jerome said. "It's his last day with us."

"Let's hope it's not his last day *period*," Ivy said.

"Don't even think it!"

Ivy let them into the closed market. Jerome hurried to the Captain's tank while Ivy stopped to grab a handful of shrimp. She offered some to Jerome.

He wrinkled his nose but then took the raw shrimp and fed them to the lobster.

"There you go, Captain," he said, wiping his hands on his pants. "By tomorrow night you'll be catching your own."

An empty feeling filled Ivy's stomach. "That's only if we win," she said.

"Of course we're going to win," Jerome said. "Look at the tickets we've collected. We can't miss!"

Ivy pulled Jerome away from the tank. "Just to be sure, let's collect some more."

By afternoon they had added twenty-two tickets to Jerome's shoe box.

"That makes a grand total of three hundred and sixty-four!" he said.

Ivy marveled at the neat stacks of tickets, all bound with rubber bands. "But how are you going to tell if we've won? It's going to take forever to look through all those."

"Relax," Jerome said. "They're all in order. It'll only take me a minute to find the winner."

He put the top on the box and tucked it under his arm. "Let's go," he said. "It's almost time for the raffle."

When they got to the park, at least half the town was in front of the picnic pavilion, where the drawing would take place. Ivy and Jerome wiggled to the front of the crowd.

Mr. Higgins gave them a wave before he turned to talk to the mayor, who was to choose the winner.

Ivy tried to keep her eyes off the gleaming cooker, but it was hard to ignore.

Jerome looked at the huge pot. "They'll have to make potato soup in it."

Ivy smiled, but a shiver went up her back.

The crowd hushed as the mayor approached the microphone. "You all know what we're here for," he said, "so let's get to it." He plunged his pudgy hand into the glass bowl and stirred the hundreds of ticket stubs around. Then he drew one out. "Number 68930," he read.

Jerome already had the lid off his box. But before he could even look, Ivy heard a shrill voice from the back of the crowd. "I won! I won!" a woman shouted.

CHAPTER 10

N̲o!" Ivy yelled. "He's almost a hundred years old. You can't do this!"

No one heard her over the mayor's blaring voice.

"Mrs. Flemming. Congratulations! We'll see you and your guests back here at six."

Mrs. Flemming, a thin woman with white hair, had run up to the platform with her ticket stub. "I've never won *anything* before," she said. "Not ever!" And her happy face was shiny with tears.

As the crowd broke up, people began to drift toward the booming music that came from the carnival rides at the far end of the park.

Ivy ran to the platform. "Wait!" she shouted. But no one was listening.

Ivy stiffened as she felt her father's hands on her shoulders.

"I'm sorry, Ivy. It's over," he said quietly.

Ivy looked for Jerome. He wasn't there. The box of ticket stubs lay spilled on the grass.

"Come on," her father said. "Let's get out of here."

Ivy was silent on the ride home. She didn't even bother to hide in her seat. She just sat there, her mind working furiously. Everyone had given up. She couldn't believe it. There had to be something else she could do!

She phoned Jerome. " I have another plan," she said. And by five-thirty she was back in the park. Her entire class was there. Some kids had brought their parents and friends, and everyone was carrying a sign.

SAVE CAPTAIN NEMO! some said. ANIMALS

HAVE RIGHTS, TOO! said others. With Ivy leading the way, they marched to the picnic pavilion, where Mrs. Flemming and her family had gathered for the clambake. Ivy's father was tending the fire under the huge cook pot. The Captain sat nearby in a large box of ice.

Ivy's father looked surprised as the crowd of children began to march around the pavilion.

"Ivy, you shouldn't be here," he said.

But Ivy pretended not to hear. Her voice picked up the chant, and her body marched along in rhythm.

"Free Captain Nemo! Free Captain Nemo!" Soon the chant and the march were the only things in her mind. For a few moments she even lost track of why she was there. The only thing she was aware of was the bouncing 94 on Jerome's shirt in front of her. So when Mrs. Flemming stopped her, Ivy was confused.

"It's okay, Ivy," Mrs. Flemming said. "We're not going to cook the Captain."

"Huh?" said Ivy.

"They're not going to eat the Captain!" Jerome

yelled in her ear.

Ivy looked around. The kids were cheering, and Mrs. Flemming had tears in her eyes.

"I talked to your father," she said. "The Captain deserves a better fate than being dipped in butter. No one will mind if we just eat clams and corn. You don't have any pet clams, do you?"

Ivy shook her head. It was over, and she had won! But not with a lucky ticket or because someone else had fought her battles, but because she had worked hard—and for once hadn't been afraid to speak up.

But she still had one more thing to do.

The sea was like a sheet of glass the next morning as Tom Robinson's fshing boat slipped out of Rocky Cove. The pungent odors of fish and diesel oil stung Ivy's nose, but Jerome didn't seem to notice.

The lobster was wrapped in wet burlap, and Ivy and Jerome knelt by his side.

They rode out past Barry's Island to open water. The engine throbbed steadily, and the rising sun turned the sea to gold. A single gull hovered overhead.

Tom Robinson cut the engine. The quiet was startling. Ivy began to remove the burlap covering from the Captain, then stopped and wiped her eyes. Jerome squeezed her hand and finished removing the burlap. Then Tom hoisted the lobster over the side and into the sea. With a single splash, the Captain was home.